NANCY CLANCY

Super Sleuth

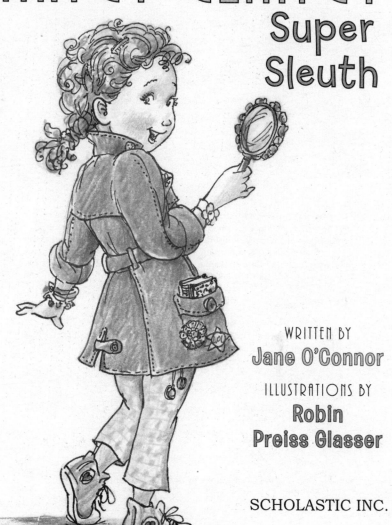

WRITTEN BY
Jane O'Connor

ILLUSTRATIONS BY
Robin Preiss Glasser

SCHOLASTIC INC.

For my superb mother-in-law, Marge O'Connor
—J.O'C.

For Aaron: alias, Mr. Dude
—R.P.G.: alias, A.O.

ISBN 978-0-545-85503-7

12 11 10 9 8 7 6 5 4 3 2 1   15 16 17 18 19 20/0

Printed in the U.S.A.   40

First Scholastic printing, March 2015

Typography by Jeanne L. Hogle

CONTENTS

CHAPTER 1: **HARDLY A MYSTERY** 1

CHAPTER 2: **SNOOPING** 7

CHAPTER 3: **THE PLOT THICKENS** 13

CHAPTER 4: **MYSTERY MEMENTOS** 29

CHAPTER 5: **THE RETURN OF RHONDA** 41

CHAPTER 6: **CRIME SCENE** 49

CHAPTER 7: **HUNTING FOR CLUES** 65

CHAPTER 8: **FINGERPRINTS** 71

CHAPTER 9: **INNOCENT!** 83

CHAPTER 10: **SUSPECTS** 95

CHAPTER 11: **CONFESSION** 101

CHAPTER 12: **CRIME AND PUNISHMENT** 111

CHAPTER 13: **CASE CLOSED** 121

CHAPTER 1

HARDLY A MYSTERY

Nancy Clancy was all set to solve a mystery. She had a fancy magnifying glass complete with rhinestones. She had a spiral notepad and a flashlight. She had sunglasses, a hat with a floppy brim, and a pink trench coat. (A trench coat was the kind of raincoat that detectives wore.) She had superb detective skills. She was naturally nosy. So she was good at snooping. (Investigating was the professional word for snooping.)

Really the only thing Nancy was missing was a mystery.

"If only more criminals lived around here," she said to her father. He was at the kitchen table reading the Sunday sports pages.

"What?" he said without looking up.

"Nobody ever gets kidnapped. I bet there's never been a jewel heist." Then, in case her dad didn't know, Nancy added, "That means a jewel robbery."

Nancy sighed. "I wish we lived someplace like River Heights." That was where Nancy Drew lived. Nancy loved the Nancy

Drew books. She had read five so far. "In River Heights, criminals are lurking around every·corner."

"Mmmmm. Sounds fun," her dad murmured.

Nancy's mother came into the kitchen. Nancy's little sister trailed behind her. She had on blue flippers that made a slapping sound as she walked.

"Have either of you seen JoJo's snorkel mask?" Nancy's mom asked.

Nancy's little sister hardly ever took off her snorkel mask or flippers. JoJo and her friend Freddy liked to pretend they were deep-sea divers searching for buried treasure.

Nancy's mom poured herself coffee. "We've looked everywhere. It's a mystery where it went."

Mystery! Nancy just heard the magic word. Okay, so it wasn't a big-deal mystery. But all great detectives had to start somewhere. She spread her arms. "Ta-da! Nancy Clancy, Super Sleuth, at your service."

"Aw, honey." Her mom smiled. "You'll look for it?"

"Sure. My rates are very reasonable." Nancy paused. "Only kidding. You're family. So my services are free."

Nancy went and slipped on her pink trench coat. It was important to dress like a professional. "JoJo, I just need to ask you a few questions," she said, pulling the notepad from her pocket. "Trust me. We'll get to the bottom of this."

At that moment, Bree appeared at the back door. She was wearing a trench coat too. (Hers was purple.)

"JoJo left this at our house." Bree was holding a snorkel mask.

"Thanks!" Nancy's mom said. Then she turned to Nancy. "Sorry, sweetie."

Nancy scowled. Her first case was closed before it even got opened.

"I have to pick up a book for my mother. It's at the twins' house," Bree told Nancy. "Come with me."

CHAPTER 2

SNOOPING

The book for Bree's mom was in the Polskys' mailbox. Nancy and Bree were about to walk back home when Bree held a finger to her lips. "Shh. Listen."

Nancy could hear the Polsky twins arguing in their backyard.

"No fair!" Wanda shouted. "I get to pitch now."

7

"No! It's still my turn!" Rhonda said.

"Is not!"

Rhonda and Wanda were a year younger than Nancy and Bree. They were both superb at sports and very nice—except to each other. They got into lots of fights. Not just yelling fights, but hitting fights.

"Let's investigate!" Nancy said. She looked around. "The coast is clear!"

The girls dropped to their knees and crawled to the side of the twins' house. They tiptoed along the wall, their backs pressed flat against it. Silent as cats, they stopped at the back porch and hid behind an outdoor grill. Neither twin had spotted them. It was like Nancy and Bree were invisible. They smiled and high-fived each other.

"Here comes my fastball." Rhonda

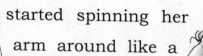

started spinning her
arm around like a
pinwheel.

"I quit."
Wanda threw
down her mitt.

"I'm not playing anymore."
She started to stomp off.

Rhonda spun her arm around once
more and let go of the ball.

Just in time, Wanda saw the ball whizzing right at her. She sprang forward to
catch it.

Oops! She missed.

Double oops! She stumbled and landed
facedown on the ground.

Ooh! That had to hurt! Nancy peeked
over the top of the grill. "Wanda's bleeding!

She split her lip."

"I can't look." Bree stayed hunched down. She hated the sight of blood.

Nancy watched Wanda pull herself up. She was crying. Blood was all over her mouth and chin. Her hands, too. Wanda looked like something out of a horror movie!

"You did that on purpose!" Wanda yelled at Rhonda. "I'm gonna get you back. I'm— I'm gonna tell Nancy what you did the other day!"

Rhonda froze for a second.

Nancy did too.

"You swore you wouldn't tell!" Rhonda shouted.

"Tough. I'm telling Nancy."

Nancy wanted to pop up from behind the grill and shout, "Tell me what?" But Bree grabbed her by the arm and yanked her down.

"We're snooping, remember?" Bree hissed.

A moment later, the twins' dad appeared on the back porch. He looked mad. "Are you two fighting again?" he said. Then he took each of them by the arm and marched them inside the house.

CHAPTER **3**

THE PLOT THICKENS

"So? What is Rhonda scared I'll find out? What secret has Wanda been keeping?" Nancy made her voice go soft and spooky. "It's the secret of the twins." She giggled. "Doesn't it sound like a Nancy Drew mystery?"

The girls were in Nancy's backyard at

Sleuth Headquarters. When they grew up, they planned to open a detective agency together. It would be called Partners in Crime Fighting. They had made superb business cards already.

"Maybe Rhonda spread a mean rumor about you," Bree said. "Like you smell or have cooties."

"Rhonda's my friend. What motive would she have?" Ooh la la! Nancy felt all tingly just saying the word "motive." It meant the reason for doing something bad.

"W-e-l-l." Bree drew the word out, like she was thinking really hard. "Maybe you did something mean to Rhonda and she's paying you back."

Nancy shook her head. "I didn't do anything."

"Maybe it's something you don't even realize you did. But it got Rhonda mad. Really mad."

"And so now Rhonda is seeking revenge?" Nancy added.

Bree nodded.

Double ooh la la! Nancy's eyes lit up. There was something thrilling about this idea. "Maybe she's set up a booby trap to get me!" Nancy pictured Rhonda digging a deep hole in her yard and covering it with

grass and branches. As soon as Nancy walked over it, she'd plunge into darkness. No one would hear her cries for help.

Suddenly Nancy heard her mother calling her.

"Nancy, are you in the clubhouse?"

Nancy stuck her head out. "Mom, I told you before. It's not our clubhouse anymore. It's Sleuth Headquarters."

"Sorry. I forgot. Have you finished your paragraph for tomorrow?"

"Um, not exactly," Nancy answered.

"Have you started it?"

"Um, not exactly."

"Bree, I'm afraid you'll have to go home, and Nancy"—Nancy's mother pointed to the house—"get cracking!"

Nancy headed to her room. Nancy Drew

was so lucky. She never had to drop a case because of homework.

Tomorrow Nancy and all the other kids in her class had to bring in something special. "A memento" was what her teacher, Mr. Dudeny, had called it. The memento couldn't be a video game or a new pair of sneakers. A memento needed to be something personal, like a photo of a dead person in your family from long ago.

"Write a paragraph about what the memento means to you. But don't sign your name," Mr. Dudeny said. "Keep it a secret. We'll have fun guessing who each memento belongs to."

"Oh! So they'll be mystery mementos," Nancy said.

"Exactly," Mr. Dude told her. "I'm

bringing something too. Then on Tuesday all the mystery mementos will be on display for Family Day."

Nancy planned to bring *The Witch Tree Symbol,* which was a Nancy Drew book. It was special because long ago it had belonged to Nancy's neighbor, Mrs. DeVine. On the cover Nancy Drew looked different. Her clothes and hairdo were old-fashioned.

The only problem was that Nancy wanted her memento to be unique— something nobody else had. What if Bree's mystery memento was the Nancy Drew book that Mrs. DeVine had given *her?* Bree had already written her paragraph days ago. She never left homework for the last minute.

So Nancy sent a message to Bree in their Top-Secret Special Delivery mailbox. It was a basket on a rope strung between Nancy's bedroom window and Bree's.

What is your memento? She wrote the message in secret code. Only the two of them knew it. They needed a secret code if one of them was ever in danger and had to send for help. Nancy rang a bell to let Bree know mail was coming. Then she

Sqqtta. Ot. F

vqnf wu Pqv

vq vgnn.

　　—Bree

pulled the rope until the basket reached Bree's window.

A few minutes later, a message came back. Bree's was in secret code too. It took Nancy a while to understand it. (In secret-code talk that was called deciphering a message.)

Bree had written: *Sorry. Mr. D told us not to tell.*

Ooh, Bree could be exasperating some-times!

Nancy thought about writing another message. But writing in code took so long. Of course, she could just pick up the phone or open the window and shout. Nancy would say, "Can you just tell me if you're bringing a Nancy Drew book? I am only asking because I don't want to bring in the same thing!"

But it wouldn't do any good. Bree was obstinate—that meant stubborn. In the end, Nancy decided to bring in a sparkling chunk of rock that looked like gold. She wanted kids to have a hard time figur-ing out who it belonged to. So when she wrote her paragraph, Nancy disguised her handwriting.

This glittering rock is called pyrite. Another name for it is fool's gold. That's because it looks like genuine gold. Long ago in days of yore, miners would find a chunk and think they had struck it rich. The joke was on them. Pyrite is not worth a lot of money. But it is still magnificent. I chose this memento because it was a present from my best friend, Bree. She bought it in a gift shop at a famous science museum in New York City.

It was quite a superb paragraph, if Nancy did say so herself. She had used

vivid, interesting words. Mr. Dudeny would like that. Then something caught Nancy's eye. In one sentence there was a dead giveaway. Everyone would know Nancy had written it. Quickly she erased the words "my best friend, Bree." Instead she wrote "an acquaintance of mine."

Nancy put the rock and her paragraph in her backpack.

Not even five minutes later, the mail bell rang again.

Bree's message said, *I just saw the twins drive off with their parents. We can go back and snoop in their yard. Maybe we'll find the booby trap!*

Nancy grabbed her trench coat. Bree was already waiting for her on the side-walk.

Bree whistled on the way over to the twins' house. Whistling was a superb detective skill. It made it seem like they were just out for some fresh air. No one would ever suspect they were snooping.

At first glance, the twins' yard looked the same as it had this morning—grass, trees, a swing set in back, lots of sports stuff everywhere. Nancy, however, was very observant. That meant she noticed stuff that other people didn't. Noticing stuff was also a superb detective skill. It kind of made up for not being able to whistle.

What Nancy noticed now was a pile of

branches near the swing set.

"Bree, look, a clue! I bet those branches are left over from when Rhonda made the booby trap!"

Bree clutched Nancy's arm. "Oh! I'm getting chills!"

A couple of large leaf rakes were on the porch. "I have an idea," Nancy said.

By pushing the rakes in front of them up and down the yard, the girls would spot the hidden trap before either of them fell into it. Unfortunately, the yard was pretty big. They hadn't covered much ground when they heard a car. It was pulling into the twins' driveway!

Bree and Nancy dropped the rakes and scrammed. They ran through the lilac bushes in between the twins' house and

Mrs. DeVine's. They dashed across Mrs. DeVine's yard, wiggled through the hedge that separated her yard from Nancy's, and hid inside Headquarters.

Whew! That was a close call. But they were safe! They collapsed into the bean-bag chairs.

"You really think there's a booby trap?" Bree asked. She sounded doubtful now.

"More and more, I'm sure of it. We need to search that whole yard. But let's sneak back under cover of darkness." That meant at night but sounded way more

dangerous. They'd have to use flash-
lights. There'd be spooky night noises.
Nancy could picture it all!

"We're not allowed out after dark," Bree
pointed out.

Nancy knew that. She just didn't want
to be reminded of it. Not right now. It was
more fun picturing the two of them sneaking around in the dark.

Nancy sighed. It was awfully difficult to
be a glamorous detective when your bed-
time was eight thirty.

CHAPTER 4

MYSTERY MEMENTOS

The cowboy hat is Robert's memento, Nancy wrote. She was filling in the blanks on her Mystery Memento sheet. Mr. Dudeny had handed a sheet to each kid. Then he said, "Go to it, Dudes."

All the mystery mementos were on a table by the windows.

The cowboy hat was easy. Robert used to live in Texas.

The glass mouse is Bree's memento, Nancy wrote.

Bree owned lots of tiny glass animals. She kept them on a special shelf in her room. *See? I knew right away. You could have told me.* Nancy didn't say those words out loud. She just thought them. Nancy figured that sometimes she and Bree could read each other's minds.

Two kids had brought in shells. One was white with brown specks. The other was white and purple. *The white-and-brown shell is Clara's memento,* Nancy wrote. Clara had not disguised her handwriting.

The paragraph for the other shell was typed. It said, *I found this shell on a beach in Florida. We stayed at a hotel with three pools. My family had a suite. Suites are bigger and cost more than regular hotel rooms. I had the best time ever in Florida.*

The white-and-purple shell had to belong to Grace. Grace bragged all the time about her trip to Florida.

"Hey! No fair, you're peeking!" Nancy said. Grace was sneaking a look at her sheet.

"I'm not! I guessed yours already," Grace said. "It's the bead bracelet."

"Maybe yes, maybe no." Nancy smiled. *Ha-ha! You are sadly mistaken. That's fancy for wrong, wrong, wrong!* Nancy didn't say this out loud either. She was not friends with Grace. Grace would never be able to read her mind.

Nancy went around the table. Hmmm. Who did the snow globe with the Statue of Liberty belong to? And what about the shark teeth? Or the swim trophy from Sighing Pines Day Camp? Nancy was stumped. She stopped at a big deep-blue marble. Bree was looking at it too. Inside it was a white swirl. The marble was taped to the table so it wouldn't fall off.

"Whose is it, you think?" Nancy said

to Bree and Clara.

"It's gorgeous," Clara said. "That's my favorite color blue."

"I bet I know who it belongs to," Grace said. "But I'm not telling."

Nancy ignored her. "It looks like a precious jewel." Nancy held up her hand and imagined the marble was a fancy ring on her finger. Then she read the paragraph.

My grandfather gave me this. He taught me how to play a game with marbles. It's a lot of fun, and I got pretty good at it. When he was a boy, all his friends played the game together. But most kids today don't know how. I can teach everybody the rules.

The paragraph talked about teaching. Was that a clue? Hmmm. Nancy tapped her pencil eraser against her lip. Maybe the marble belonged to Mr. Dudeny.

At the end of the day, the kids revealed which mementos were theirs.

"Mine is the potato that looks like a witch's head," Lionel said.

"I knew it!" lots of kids said at once. Nancy had guessed right too. Lionel was such a goofball.

Besides Bree, only Robert and Tamar figured out Nancy's memento. The other kids probably figured she'd bring in something fancier.

Mr. Dudeny went last. "I brought in the marble."

"Superb!" Nancy punched her fist in the air. "I guessed it was yours, Mr. D."

Grace said, "I got thirteen right. That's really good, isn't it, Mr. Dude?"

"This isn't a test," Mr. Dudeny said. "Guessing was just for fun. Your paragraphs are enthralling. That means I found them very, very interesting. So, Dudes? Want to learn how to play marbles?"

Everybody crowded around Mr. Dudeny while he drew a chalk circle on the floor.

In the middle he made a plus sign with thirteen smaller marbles.

He held up the big blue marble. "This is the shooter. It shoots the little marbles."

"Hey, I'm a marble. Ooh! Ooh! I got shot!" Lionel clutched his chest and staggered around.

"If you shoot a marble outside the circle, you get a point," Mr. D explained. "The player with the most points wins.

I used to be pretty good."

He bent down on one knee. He put his blue shooter outside the circle. A flick of his thumb sent it whizzing toward the little marbles. Three got hit. When they stopped rolling, two were outside the circle.

"Ooh. Can we try?" Robert asked.

Mr. Dudeny said, "It just so happens I brought a bunch of shooters." He started handing them out. Robert got one with

orange stripes. Lionel got one that looked like a bloodshot eyeball. Nancy got a green shooter with sparkles inside.

"No fair! Yours is prettier than mine," Grace said to Nancy, and pushed in front of her. "Can I go first, Mr. D? Can I?"

"Whoa, no pushing. Everybody will get a turn."

Shooting marbles was harder than it looked. Nancy didn't get any points.

"Don't feel bad," Bree said. "I stink too."

When it was almost time to go home, Mr. D scooped up the little marbles. Then he passed a bag around to collect the shooters.

"Hey! Watch this." Lionel held the eyeball marble between his thumb and his pointer finger. He made a fist and rubbed both his hands together. When he opened them, the eyeball marble was gone.

"Pretty good trick!" their teacher said.

"It's not a trick," Lionel insisted. "It's magic."

"Then do some more magic and make it reappear." Mr. Dudeny waited until Lionel dug inside his sleeve for the marble.

"Aw, rats," said Lionel. "I wanted to keep it."

Mr. Dudeny was retaping the beautiful blue shooter to the table when the bell rang.

"Adios, Dudes. See you tomorrow on Family Day."

CHAPTER 5

THE RETURN OF RHONDA

Before dinner, Nancy was at Headquarters. She was reading about how
to make disappearing ink. Suddenly the
curtain parted. She expected to see Bree.
Instead, there was Rhonda.

"Uh, hi, Nancy. Your mom said you were

out here. Um, look, I"—Rhonda shifted from leg to leg—"I came over to tell you something."

Well, this was an interesting development! Had Rhonda come to confess?

Nancy smiled an encouraging smile. She waited for Rhonda to drop to her knees and start sobbing about the horrible thing she'd done. And because Nancy was so kindhearted, she'd say, "Of course I forgive you, Rhonda."

"Uh, look, Nancy . . ." Rhonda seemed about to blurt something out but then stopped. When she spoke, all she said was, "Want to come over and play soccer? My dad just set up a goal in our yard."

What? So Rhonda wasn't here to confess? Then she must have come over to lure Nancy into the trap!

"It'll be fun," Rhonda said.

Oh, right! It'll be a ton of fun to fall into some hole you dug. So a hundred years from now, a kid will be playing in your yard and discover a bunch of bones—my bones!

"No," Nancy said. "Maybe some other time." *As in, never!*

"Well, then—uh, bye, I guess," Rhonda said.

"No, wait!" Nancy pulled Rhonda inside and sat her in one of the beanbag chairs. Now was her chance to make Rhonda talk.

"Stay. Have a snack." She handed Rhonda a bag of cookies. On TV shows detectives sometimes got suspects to blab by acting really friendly. Nancy figured she'd give it a try.

"It sure is great to see you, Rhonda," Nancy said.

"Huh? You see me all the time." Rhonda nibbled on a cookie.

"I know. But it's always great." Nancy paused. "That's because we're friends, right?"

"Yeah, sure." She took another cookie

and stood up. "I better get home."

Nancy had to think fast.

"Look, Rhonda. I don't think you came here because you wanted to play soccer. Tell me why you really came over."

Rhonda avoided Nancy's eyes. "I—I don't know what you're talking about."

"Oh, I think you do," Nancy said.

Suddenly Rhonda slumped back down in the beanbag chair. Nancy poured a glass of water and handed it to her.

"Make it easy on yourself, Rhonda, and tell me the real reason you came over. I can tell you want to confess."

Rhonda took a sip. "Well—" She started to speak when Nancy's mother barged into Headquarters.

"Your mom called," she told Rhonda. "She wants you home."

Rhonda sprang from the chair. "See you!" she cried, and was gone.

"I was working on a case, Mom. I was about to crack it wide open when you came in."

"My bad, Sherlock. . . . Listen. I bought strawberries for dessert. Want to help make whipped cream?"

"I guess." Nancy followed her mother to the kitchen. How come Nancy Drew never ran into the problems that Nancy Clancy did, trying to solve a mystery?

Of course, Nancy Drew didn't have a mother. There was just her father, Carson Drew, and a kindly housekeeper named Hannah. Nancy felt sorry for Nancy Drew not having a mother. But maybe Mrs. Drew would have messed up her cases too.

CHAPTER 6

CRIME SCENE

"Hurry, honey!" Nancy's mom called.

"Mom, I can't find one of my bracelets." Nancy needed it to complete her outfit for Family Day.

"Really. It's time to go," her mom said. "We don't want to be late."

Nancy came downstairs, and right away

she saw the bracelet she'd been looking for.

It was on JoJo's wrist.

Nancy pointed. "That's my bracelet!"

"Sorry!" JoJo said. Right away, she took off the bracelet and went to get her jacket.

"She always takes stuff without asking," Nancy said to her parents.

"Don't be mad, Nancy." JoJo clasped her hands together. "Please don't be mad."

"Okay, okay," Nancy said.

On the walk to school, JoJo slipped her hand into Nancy's and skipped the whole way.

The Clancys were among the first to arrive in room 3D. After saying hi to Mr. D, Nancy steered her parents to the mementos table.

"Voilà!" She pointed to her chunk of pyrite. "I hope you'll find my paragraph enthralling."

Before long, the classroom filled up with families. Bree had brought a disposable camera. So Nancy posed like a model by her chunk of fool's gold. Then Nancy took a photo of Bree with her glass

mouse. Then Bree took a photo of JoJo
and Freddy together.

Lionel was dragging his parents over to
see the witch potato.

"Smile, Lionel," Bree said.

"Wait!" Lionel said, holding up the
potato. "Okay, now!" Lionel's tongue
was hanging down on his chin. His eyes
were rolled so far back, all you could

see were the whites.

"Stop that, Lionel!" his mother scolded.
"Nobody else is acting silly."

Nancy's mom and dad looked at each
other and smiled.

"What?" Nancy asked.

Her father nodded at Lionel. "That
was me, twenty-five years ago. The class
clown."

Bree snapped more pictures of kids and their mementos. Then they joined a bunch of kids at the snack table while Mr. Dudeny talked to the parents.

"I am so glad we could share our mementos with you," he said. "This is part of our unit on families. Earlier in the year, we made family trees. Soon each child will begin writing an autobiography. In art they will make family collages, and in . . ."

Nancy tuned out the rest of what Mr. Dudeny was saying. She watched JoJo and smiled. JoJo was taking Yoko's little sister around the memento table. Hariko was only three. JoJo was holding her hand and pointing out different stuff to her. It was like JoJo was pretending to be a big sister.

Deep down, Nancy was glad JoJo had come to Family Day. She hugged her sister when it was time for all the families to leave.

"Au revoir!" Nancy said, waving.

Bree kept snapping photos all day—at lunch, in the school yard, during art, and lots more in their classroom.

"One left," she said. Her desk was next to Nancy's.

"Take another of me." Nancy had her creative-writing journal out. She put a dreamy look on her face and held a pencil with her pinky finger up. "Do I look creative?"

"Bree!" Mr. Dudeny said. "Please put the camera away and get to work."

Nancy loved creative writing. She was writing a mystery called "The Vanishing Jewel." It starred a young detective named Lucette Fromage. Lucette had long, curly tresses. "Tresses" was such a beautiful word for hair. Lucette was also the same age as Nancy.

Lucette Fromage sprinted after the robbers, Nancy wrote. Mr. Dudeny liked vivid—that meant colorful—words. "Sprinted" was way more vivid than "ran."

"Be careful, Lucette Fromage!" the countess shouted from the steps of her mansion. "My sapphire blue ring is priceless. But I don't want you to get maimed."

The robbers laughed like maniacs. "You'll never catch us!" Then they drove off in an ugly used car.

It was hard trying to write the chase scene. Lucette was too young to drive. Ah! Nancy decided to give Lucette really fast, strong legs. *Lucette hopped on her bike and began pedaling at seventy miles an hour,* Nancy wrote. *Soon she was right behind the robbers.*

At one point, Nancy turned around and looked up. Mr. Dudeny was standing behind her desk. He was reading over her shoulder. "Superb!" he said.

"Dudes, listen to all the vivid words Nancy has used," Mr Dudeny said.

Nancy read out loud to the class. She explained that "priceless" meant really expensive and "maimed" meant hurt. Then she said, "At first I was going to make the stolen ring be a diamond ring. But I changed it to a sapphire after seeing Mr. Dudeny's beautiful blue marble."

"Hey! Look!" Grace said in surprise. She was pointing to the mementos table.

The crisscrossed pieces of tape were still stuck on the table. But the marble was gone.

"No worries. It must have gotten unstuck and rolled off," Mr. Dudeny said. "Let's search."

Grace checked the wastebaskets. Yoko, Lionel, and Tamar went through the book bins in case the marble had dropped into one. Nancy and Bree searched under the radiators. Nancy saw a dead bug, but no marble.

"It's not in Eric Clapton's cage, either," Clara said. "I checked."

Grace rolled her eyes. "Cla-ra! How could that huge marble get inside the hamster's cage?"

"I don't know. But I checked anyway." Clara looked upset. "How could it have disappeared?"

"I'm sure it'll turn up," Mr. Dudeny

kept saying.

"I think somebody stole it!" Grace said, in a low voice so Mr. D couldn't hear.

"You think she's right?" Nancy asked Bree.

"It does seem suspicious."

"Then our classroom might be a crime scene!" This struck Nancy as both thrilling and upsetting.

Right before going home, Bree aimed her camera at the mementos table. "Maybe we can get the pictures back today." She paused and snapped her last picture. "Who knows? There could be a clue!"

Ooh la la! Now Nancy and Bree had two mysteries to solve—the Secret of the Twins . . . and the Case of the Missing Marble!

CHAPTER 7

HUNTING
FOR CLUES

Bree's mom came back with the photos late that afternoon. The girls looked through them at Sleuth Headquarters.

Bree giggled. "Look at Lionel."

Nancy was busy studying some other photos. "I am trying to establish the time of the crime." In sleuth talk, establish meant figuring out something.

"These two photos are clues." Nancy handed Bree one of Bree's parents at the display table. "See the clock on the wall?"

"Yeah. It says eleven," Bree said.

"The blue marble is still there." Nancy held up a different photo. "Now look." Everybody except Bree was standing

behind the display table. Mr. Dudeny was in the photo too. But the marble was gone.

"Ooh, I have goosebumps!" Bree said.

"Me too! Too bad the clock got cut off in this one."

"Doesn't matter," Bree said. "I remember I took it right after lunch."

"Hmmm. Lunch is over at one fifteen. So that means the marble disappeared sometime between eleven and one fifteen." Nancy heard herself and stopped. "Oh, Bree! We are really sleuthing! Nancy Drew would be so proud."

Bree flung her arms around Nancy. "Partner, we are going to crack this case wide open!"

*   *   *

At dinner that evening, Nancy's dad said, "My, my. Just the other day you were complaining about the lack of crime around here." He paused to spoon some carrots onto his plate. "And now look! Grand theft at school!"

"Doug, stop teasing," her mom said.

"Looks like an inside job to me," her dad went on, ignoring a loud sigh from her mom.

"I don't feel good. My tummy hurts." JoJo climbed into Mom's lap.

Nancy's dad turned to her and said, "So? Was anybody ever alone in the classroom?"

Nancy had already thought about that. "No. Only Mr. Dudeny. He stays in while we're at recess."

"Hmmm. Doubtful he stole his own marble . . . unless, of course, your teacher is losing his marbles." Her dad laughed at his own joke. Her mother shook her head and carried JoJo upstairs to lie down until she felt better.

CHAPTER **8**

FINGERPRINTS

L ater that evening, Nancy lay on her bed, pondering. Pondering was like thinking, only fancier. Next to her on her night table was *The Witch Tree Symbol. How would Nancy Drew go about solving the Case of the Missing Marble?* she wondered.

Nancy picked up the book and opened it.

71

She didn't expect to find any answers in it. She just liked looking at the first page. In the top corner it said *Marjorie Sneff* in curly script. That had been Mrs. DeVine's name when she was a child in days of yore.

"Sacre bleu!" Nancy said out loud. In French that meant "Oh my gosh!"

There was a dark brown fingerprint by Mrs. DeVine's name. It had never been there before. And the page was torn.

"JoJo!" Nancy hollered. She charged into her sister's room. JoJo was on the floor, playing with all the things in her plastic treasure chest. Evidently her tummy felt all better. She was eating an Oreo. Dark brown crumbs were all over her mouth and fingers.

She looked up, saw Nancy, and snapped

her treasure chest shut. She had a guilty look on her face.

"You're not allowed to touch my stuff!" Nancy shoved the open book at her sister. "Look what you did!"

"I didn't do that!"

"You did too! Look at your hands. This fingerprint was made by someone eating an Oreo cookie!"

Quickly JoJo hid her hands behind her back. "It wasn't me! I don't like those books. They're scary."

Nancy ran to find their mother. She was halfway down the hall when she stopped. Maybe JoJo was telling the truth. The covers of the Nancy Drew books did scare her.

Nancy examined the fingerprint in the book more closely. It was big. It was probably a thumbprint.

"Come with me," she told JoJo. They went into Nancy's room. Nancy took her sister's hand and pressed her thumb onto a page in her detective notepad. A brown thumbprint appeared. It was the same color as the thumbprint in the Nancy Drew book. But it was much smaller.

JoJo was innocent after all.

"I'm sorry I blamed you," Nancy told her.

"That's okay," JoJo said. "Will you read to me?"

"Yeah, I guess."

They went back to

JoJo's room. JoJo pushed her treasure chest under her bed and found her favorite book. She handed it to Nancy. It was about a pirate ship and buried treasure.

The whole time Nancy was reading, she kept thinking about the brown thumbprint in her book. Who besides Bree and JoJo had been in her room lately?

Ooh la la! It hit her. The twins! They had come over a few days ago after soccer. Had Rhonda been eating anything chocolatey? No, Nancy didn't think so. But maybe the thumbprint wasn't chocolate. Maybe it was dirt! That made sense. Everybody came back from soccer all muddy. Nancy never would have let Rhonda touch the Nancy Drew book with dirty hands. So when did Rhonda commit the crime?

Suddenly Nancy remembered. Mrs. DeVine had called about coming for tea. While Nancy was on the phone, the twins were alone in her room. Double ooh la la! All the pieces of the puzzle were falling into place. Rhonda had probably picked up the Nancy Drew book just to look at it, and messed it up by mistake. Rhonda was scared to confess. And so Rhonda made Wanda promise not to tell Nancy.

It all made sense. Still, Nancy had no proof. On TV, detectives always talked about fingerprint files. If a fingerprint was found at the scene of a crime, they could match it up with one in the files.

The trouble was, Nancy didn't have any other fingerprints of Rhonda's. . . .

Or did she? Rhonda had been at

Headquarters just yesterday. The glass of water!

Nancy flew downstairs.

"Wait! You didn't finish!" JoJo called.

Nancy grabbed her trench coat and a flashlight from the pantry. Her father was loading stuff into the dishwasher.

"Where are you going?"

"To Headquarters. I'll be right back."

Outside, Nancy clicked on the flashlight. She made her way under cover of darkness. Inside Headquarters, the glow from the flashlight cast spooky shadows.

There it was. The plastic glass with Tinker Bell on it. Nancy held it at the bottom so she wouldn't get her own prints on it.

Once she was back in the kitchen,

she put the Tinker Bell glass on a counter. Then she turned to her father. "Dad, whatever you do, don't touch that glass! It's evidence!"

"Whew! Lucky you warned me!" he said.

There was no time for the Special Delivery mail basket. Nancy called Bree. She filled her in, then asked, "See if your mom will let you come over. And bring the kit!"

Bree's aunt had sent her a Junior

Detective kit for her birthday. It had all sorts of superb stuff, including a bottle of fingerprint powder.

"This is so thrilling!" Bree said as she burst into the Clancys' kitchen. "I can't believe we're going to dust for prints."

Nancy's father stood by, watching. "Whatever it is, I swear I'm innocent! I'm a law-abiding man with a wife and children."

"Very funny, Dad," Nancy said as he left the room. She put on a pair of yellow rubber kitchen gloves. "This way no more prints will get on the glass." Very carefully she picked up the Tinker Bell glass. Bree sprinkled on some fingerprint powder.

Sure enough, five white, powdery fingerprints appeared. Bree was peering at the biggest one with the little magnifying glass from her kit. "Here's the thumbprint."

They took the glass upstairs. Nancy showed Bree the brown fingerprint in her

Nancy Drew book.

"Now comes the test," Nancy said. Using her jeweled magnifying glass, she studied both thumbprints. So did Bree.

"Definitely a match!" Nancy said. "The thumbprints are identical! We have solved the Secret of the Twins. Just like real detectives."

Bree said, "So what happens next?"

The answer was obvious. "We solve the Case of the Missing Marble!" Nancy said.

"No, that's not what I meant. Will you confront Rhonda with the evidence?"

"Oh!" Nancy sank down onto her bed. "I have to think about it. . . . Rhonda should have just told me. I would have been mad. But not that mad."

CHAPTER **9**

INNOCENT!

Nancy's mom was wrong about the janitor finding Mr. Dudeny's blue marble.

"Still missing," Mr. D said when Nancy asked the next morning.

The missing marble was all anybody

could talk about before the bell rang.

"Dudes, come on! It is only a marble," Mr. D told the class.

"But it was your mystery memento!" Yoko said.

"It was very beautiful!" Clara said.

"Your grandpa gave it to you!" Robert said. "That's important."

"The memories I have of my grandfather are what's most important. I'll have those forever. Listen. I hope the marble turns up. But let's not overreact. . . . Now please get out your spelling books."

Nancy opened her desk to get her book. Instead she got a nasty surprise.

There was a piece of lined paper with a message.

I THINK YOU STOLE THE MARBLE!

Nancy was so shocked, she jumped back in her seat.

"What? Is there a mouse?" Clara asked.

Nancy didn't answer. She was still staring at the note. How dare someone accuse her of stealing!

Mr. Dudeny came over to her. "Is something wrong?"

Nancy nodded.

Mr. Dudeny took her outside into the hall.

Nancy showed him the message. It was written in green marker in big capital letters. The marker was going dry, so the letters looked like they were disappearing. It made the message look even meaner, and scarier, too.

Mr. Dude's lips were pressed together tightly.

"I swear I didn't take it, Mr. D!" Nancy felt tears start to prick her eyes.

"Nancy, of course you didn't. I don't think anybody took it. But I'd never, ever think that of you. You are a girl with a lot of integrity."

"*Merci*, Mr. D." She wasn't sure what integrity meant. But she could tell it was good.

After she returned to her seat, Mr. Dudeny held up the message. "This was in Nancy's desk."

Several kids gasped.

"Oh! That's so mean!" Clara said.

"Nancy is innocent!" Bree cried. She reached over and squeezed Nancy's hand.

"Clara is right. This is very hurtful. From

the first day of school, we have talked about respecting one another's feelings. I expect the person who wrote this to come see me before the end of the day." Then Mr. Dudeny put the note in his desk.

He told the class to put away their spelling books. Instead, he got one of the books from the reading nook. "It's called *Thick and Thin*. And it's about friends trusting one another."

The story was about a boy who got into trouble after finding a twenty-dollar bill in a parking lot. Nancy couldn't pay attention. She kept saying to herself, *Somebody thinks I'm a thief.*

At one point Mr. Dudeny looked up from the book and said, "Grace, please stop doodling and listen."

"I am. I can do both at once," Grace answered.

Mr. Dudeny went over to Grace's desk. He crumpled up the piece of paper and tossed it into the wastebasket. Then he picked up the book again.

Throughout the morning, Nancy kept thinking about the message. By the time it was recess, she was way more than mad. She was furious. She felt outraged!

"Come on," Bree said. "If we run we can claim the top of the jungle gym before the fourth graders get it."

"Go ahead. I'll come in a second."

The classroom cleared out fast. Mr. Dudeny was at Clara's desk, going over her math problems. Clara often needed extra help.

On the way out, something made Nancy fish the crumpled piece of paper from the wastebasket. It was just a hunch.

Grace's doodles were in green marker. The marker was almost all dried out.

Nancy stormed outside to the yard. She spotted Grace over near the slides. She was jumping rope. A bunch of first graders were watching her and counting off the jumps.

"Sixteen . . . seventeen . . . eighteen . . ."

Nancy waited until Grace lost her turn. Then Nancy cornered her. "It was you! You stuck that mean note in my desk!"

Grace blinked. "Says who?"

"Me. This"—Nancy shoved the doodle at Grace—"and the note are both in green marker, a green marker that is almost dry."

Grace looked caught for a second. Then she said, "Well—well, I wasn't trying to cover it up, so there. I don't care if you know it's me. I still think you're the thief."

"Why didn't you just say it to my face?" Then Nancy paused. "What makes you think I took it?"

"You kept saying how beautiful the marble was. . . . And that story you wrote, about the sapphire ring that got stolen."

Even to Nancy, it kind of made sense that Grace figured she was the thief.

"You wanted Mr. D's marble. So you took it!"

"I did not, Grace. Who knows? Maybe you did. And—and you're just trying to throw the blame on me."

Grace's mouth dropped open.

Ha! Got you, Nancy said to herself. Yet she didn't like how hard and mean she sounded.

"That's crazy!" Grace said. Her hands were on her hips. "Some dumb baby marble. Why would I want it?" Then all of a sudden Grace got a funny look on her face. "Are you going to blab to Mr. Dudeny about me putting the note in your desk?"

"I'm not a tattletale. But you better tell him."

Grace shrugged. "Okay." Then she went back to wait for another turn at jump rope. Grace was an expert at jumping rope. She could do a perfect split. She was a great speller. And she never lost blinking contests. Still, Nancy wouldn't ever want to trade places with Grace.

"Nancy! Over here!" Bree, Tamar, and Clara called from the top of the jungle gym.

Nancy ran off to join her friends.

CHAPTER **10**

SUSPECTS

"Okay. Let's get down to business," Bree said that afternoon. "We need to draw up a list of suspects."

They were in Bree's room. Nancy was staying at Bree's until her mom and JoJo came home.

WHO STOLE THE BLUE MARBLE? Bree wrote at the top of a page in her notepad. Bree had gorgeous handwriting—her capital Bs were especially lovely.

Lionel, Bree wrote. She looked up at Nancy. "I put him down because he likes to play tricks. Maybe he took the marble as a prank."

Nancy shook her head. "Lionel wouldn't go that far. Lionel's a goofball, but I don't think he took the marble."

"Yes, you're right." Bree crossed out Lionel's name.

Nancy bit her lip and thought. On TV the crook often turned out to be the person nobody suspected. "You think maybe Clara took it?"

"Clara? That's just crazy."

"She said it was beautiful and her favorite color. . . . Who knows? Maybe some evil
force came over Clara and she was power-
less to stop herself." Nancy made her hands
into claws. "Before she realized what she
was doing, Clara snatched the marble!"

"That's just crazy," Bree repeated. "Clara
never even takes a Kleenex from the box
on Mr. D's desk without asking."

"What about Grace?" Nancy and Bree
said at the same time. Then they both
shouted, "Jinx!" The rule with a jinx was
you couldn't talk until somebody said
your name. And Bree was usually very
strict about jinxes. But she agreed to for-
get about it, just this once. Solving the
case was more important.

"Bree, if I tell you something, will you

keep it in the vault?" A vault was like a
bank safe.

Bree shut her lips. Then she pretended
to turn a key and lock her mouth.

"Grace wrote that mean message about
me being the thief."

Bree gasped. "Grace is horrible. She's
the worst person in our class! I bet she
is the thief. Criminals always try to throw
the blame on somebody else. That's why
she wrote that message."

Nancy nodded. "I said that to her. And Grace was the one who first noticed the marble was missing."

"Well!" Bree threw out her arms as if that settled everything. "On TV shows, the person who reports a crime is always a prime suspect. . . . Plus, Grace cheats. Once she copied off my spelling test. Cheaters often grow up to be thieves. Grace just jumped from cheater to thief early."

Nancy had to admit, Bree was building a pretty solid case against Grace. Of course, they didn't have one major thing—evidence.

A few minutes later, Nancy heard her mom's car in the driveway.

"Gotta go," Nancy told Bree. "I really feel like we're closing in on this case."

CHAPTER **11**

CONFESSION

Nancy burst into her house.

She found her mother upstairs. She was holding a thermometer.

"Mom, you won't believe what Grace did!" Then Nancy told her the story.

"You're right. I can't believe it!" She cupped Nancy's face in her hand and kissed her forehead. Then Nancy's mom asked, "Does your teacher know about this? Maybe I should speak to Grace's parents?"

"No, don't! Grace confessed to Mr. Dudeny. He's taking care of it. He told me before I left school. You don't need to call anybody! Promise!"

"Okay, okay. I promise."

"At first I felt awful. But all day long, kids in my class kept coming up to me. They all said how they knew I'd never steal anything." Nancy paused. "I never realized I had so much integrity."

Her mom wrapped Nancy in a hug and planted another kiss on her forehead. "You sure do, kiddo!"

Nancy followed her down the hall to JoJo's room. JoJo was in bed. "Your teacher said you were fine all day." Mom bent down and stroked JoJo's cheek. Then she turned to Nancy. "As soon as we got home, JoJo started complaining again about her tummy hurting." She popped the thermometer under JoJo's tongue. "Maybe I should call Dr. Cornelia."

JoJo yanked out the thermometer. *"No!"*

A moment later, Nancy's mom read the

thermometer. "No fever. . . . Maybe a little ginger ale will make you feel better?"

"Maybe." JoJo pulled the covers up to her chin.

Nancy's mom went downstairs.

Because Nancy felt sorry for her sister, she said, "Want to look through your treasures together?" It was one of JoJo's favorite things to do. Nancy started to pull out the plastic chest from under JoJo's bed.

"*No!* Go away!"

"Fine." Nancy headed back to her own room. "I was trying to be nice."

The phone started ringing.

"Nan, would you get it?"

It was Rhonda. She didn't bother saying hello. She started talking real fast. "Nancy, I got your special Nancy Drew book dirty, the one Mrs. DeVine gave you. And the page got torn. I didn't mean to. My hands were dirty. Please don't be mad. That's why I came over the other day. I was going to tell you, but I chickened out."

"It's okay, Rhonda," Nancy broke in. "I forgive you."

"You do? Oh, wow! Oh, phew! I was so worried you'd be mad. I felt horrible about it. My mom thought I was getting sick because I was acting so weird."

Nancy understood. Guilt could do horrible things to a person.

"All I can say is I'm really, really, really sorry, Nancy."

"Apology accepted!"

Nancy hung up the phone and went back to her room. She could hear her mom in JoJo's room.

"Is something bothering you?" Mom was saying. "Is there anything you want to tell me? I won't be mad."

Suddenly Nancy had a funny feeling in *her* tummy. She was thinking about what Rhonda had just said on the phone. How Rhonda's mom thought she was sick, when really Rhonda was just feeling guilty about Nancy's book.

Nancy bolted outside to Headquarters. She sat down and leafed through Bree's photos from Family Day again. She stopped at one of JoJo holding hands with Yoko's baby sister. JoJo was pointing at the marble. The next photo was of Freddy. He was by the display table too. JoJo and Hariko were off to one side. Nancy looked

closer. JoJo was reaching for something on the table.

Nancy felt prickles on the back of her neck. Of course, the photo didn't prove anything. It wasn't evidence. Nancy put the pictures down and pondered. She thought about what Grace had said the other day: *"Why would I steal some dumb baby marble?"*

Most of all, Nancy thought about the way JoJo acted a minute ago when Nancy suggested looking through her treasure chest. Was there something inside it that JoJo didn't want Nancy to see?

It was like a bunch of arrows with blinking lights were all pointing straight at her sister. Taking Nancy's stuff was one thing. But taking someone else's stuff? That wasn't borrowing. That was stealing!

Nancy marched back into her sister's room. Their mother was gone. Nancy expected to find JoJo in bed. Instead she was on the floor, tying up one of her dolls.

"She was being bad. So I'm punishing her," JoJo said.

Nancy knelt down and fished around under JoJo's bed. She felt the treasure chest.

"Hey! What are you doing?"

Nancy didn't reply. She sat back on her

heels. Her heart started
thumping as she raised
the lid.

There it was: the blue marble.

Nancy grabbed it and charged downstairs with JoJo running after her, howling
at the top of her lungs, "Stop!"

Her father had just come through the
front door. Her mom was waiting to kiss
him hello.

"What's wrong?" they both said.

JoJo kept screaming and trying to grab
the marble from Nancy.

Nancy cleared her throat. "I'm very sorry
to inform you that JoJo stole Mr. Dudeny's
blue marble."

Then Nancy opened her hand and
revealed the evidence.

CHAPTER 12

CRIME AND PUNISHMENT

Nancy spread out the photos from Family Day on the kitchen table. "Voilà! See for yourself!" she said, pointing. "There's JoJo reaching for the marble. And here it is!"

"Nancy, JoJo's not on trial," her dad said. "So you can put away Exhibit A." JoJo was

sitting on his lap, crying and hiccuping.

"Daddy, do you think this is funny?" Nancy plopped down in a chair. She was trying to be helpful. If her parents didn't watch out, JoJo could end up behind bars. She'd get nothing to eat but stale bread and stale water. Plus there was absolutely no way to look fancy in jail clothes.

"No, it's not funny," her dad said. "But it's not the crime of the century, either."

Nancy's mom handed JoJo a glass of water. Then her mom said, "Sweetie, why did you take the marble? You know that isn't right."

JoJo nodded miserably. Twin worms of snot were dripping down her nose.

"How about you tell us what happened," her mom said.

"Nancy will yell!"

"No, she won't," said Nancy's dad, while her mom leaned over and wiped JoJo's nose with a paper napkin.

JoJo sighed a big, heavy sigh. "I was being nice," she began. "Yoko's little sister wanted to see the marble. I tried lifting her. But she was heavy. So I picked up the marble and showed it to her." JoJo shrugged.

She acted like that settled everything.

But Nancy's dad said, "And then?"

JoJo frowned. Reluctantly, she went on. "It was so pretty, like treasure. . . . I put the marble in my pocket and took it home. I wanted to keep it in my treasure chest." All of a sudden her face scrunched up again. "I'm a bad girl! I'm a very bad girl!" she cried, and covered her face with her hands.

Nancy couldn't help feeling sorry for her little sister. Maybe JoJo had been born with no integrity and couldn't help herself.

"No, you're not a bad girl," Nancy's mom said, stroking JoJo's hair. "You're a good girl, a good girl who did something wrong. But we'll fix it. Tomorrow we'll go to Nancy's school. And you'll give the marble back to her teacher."

JoJo was not happy hearing this. "I'll let Nancy give it back."

"Me! No way!"

"JoJo, you took the marble," her dad said. "So you need to give it back and tell Mr. Dudeny how sorry you are."

Well, finally a little justice, thought Nancy, though JoJo was getting off way too easily.

So, after dinner, once her sister was in bed, Nancy marched into her parents' room. "Aren't you going to punish JoJo? I think you should."

Her dad closed the book he was reading. "Exactly what did you have in mind? A year of hard labor?"

"Ha-ha, Daddy. . . . What if saying sorry doesn't stop JoJo from stealing more stuff?"

Her mother was doing a crossword puzzle. She looked up. "It stopped you."

"Me?" Nancy pointed at herself. "What are you talking about?"

Her mom put down the newspaper. "You don't remember? You once took a rhinestone hair clip that belonged to Mrs. DeVine."

"I beg your pardon. I did no such—!" Nancy stopped cold and blinked a couple of times. Ooh, actually, maybe she did remember. "Was it shaped like a bow? And did it have pink rhinestones?"

Her mother nodded. "Yep!"

The hair clip had been on Mrs. DeVine's night table. It was magnificent! Nancy remembered trying to clip it in her hair. Then, before she knew what she was doing,

116

Nancy had slipped it into her pocket and taken it home. Just like JoJo. Suddenly Nancy had a terrible thought: Maybe crime ran in the family!

"I found the hair clip under your pillow. Mrs. DeVine didn't even realize it was missing until I took you to return it."

It all came back to Nancy. "I was so scared. I thought Mrs. DeVine would never want to see me again! But she gave me a hug and we had a tea party."

"And see? Did you wind up on America's Most Wanted list? No!"

"Oh, Daddy!" Nancy said. Her father could be so exasperating. But then he came over and hugged her. "In my humble opinion, you have turned into quite a splendid girl. So maybe there's hope for your sister."

Maybe her dad was right. This was what Mr. Dudeny called "food for thought." And Nancy definitely needed to ponder it more. But first she needed to do something else.

She went to her room. After a little while, she sent the Top-Secret Special Delivery mail basket over to Bree's window. In it was a message. In secret code, Nancy had written:

Oggv og cv
jgcfswctvgtu
CUCR!

Ygct aqwt
vtgpej eqcv.

To decipher the code, see page 20.

CHAPTER **13**

"You weren't supposed to crack the case by yourself!" Bree had on her mad face. Her lips were puckered so her mouth looked like a purse with the strings pulled tight. "We're Partners in Crime Fighting. *Partners*—that means we do stuff together."

Nancy was startled. This was not the reaction she expected. "Bree. I didn't mean to. Looking at your photos again made everything click."

Bree still looked mad.

"I'm sorry I solved the case alone," Nancy went on. "It was scary opening JoJo's treasure chest. Seeing that marble freaked me out! I wish you'd been there."

Bree's lips unpuckered a little. "The photos really were a clue?"

"A superb clue." Then Nancy said, "I bet you'll crack our next case. Then we'll be even."

Bree nodded. She was quiet for a moment. It was clear that she was pondering something. Then she said, "I'm happy JoJo turned out to be the culprit."

Now Nancy got angry. "Well, *merci* a bunch!"

"Wait. I'm not being mean," Bree answered. "But it was creepy thinking somebody in our class was a thief." She shuddered a little.

Okay, now Nancy understood. "Yes. I didn't even want it to be Grace."

Grace! Nancy would die—she would absolutely expire—if Grace found out about JoJo. Nancy's mother planned to call Mr. Dudeny tonight. She promised Nancy that JoJo would confess tomorrow after everybody in the class had gone home.

"Bree, you are the only person I'm telling. My parents said I could because you are like family. But you have to swear up and down not to tell anyone."

"It's in the vault." Bree locked her lips with a pretend key.

Then they hugged and said, *"Bonsoir, chérie,"* which was French for "Good night, darling."

As they left Headquarters, Bree said, "In Nancy Drew, some evil-looking stranger always turns out to be the criminal. It's easy to tell who's bad because they've got ugly scars or sneer a lot. It's never a cute little kid like JoJo. And it would never, never be anyone in Nancy Drew's family."

Nancy Clancy giggled. "Of course not. Nancy Drew is an only child!"